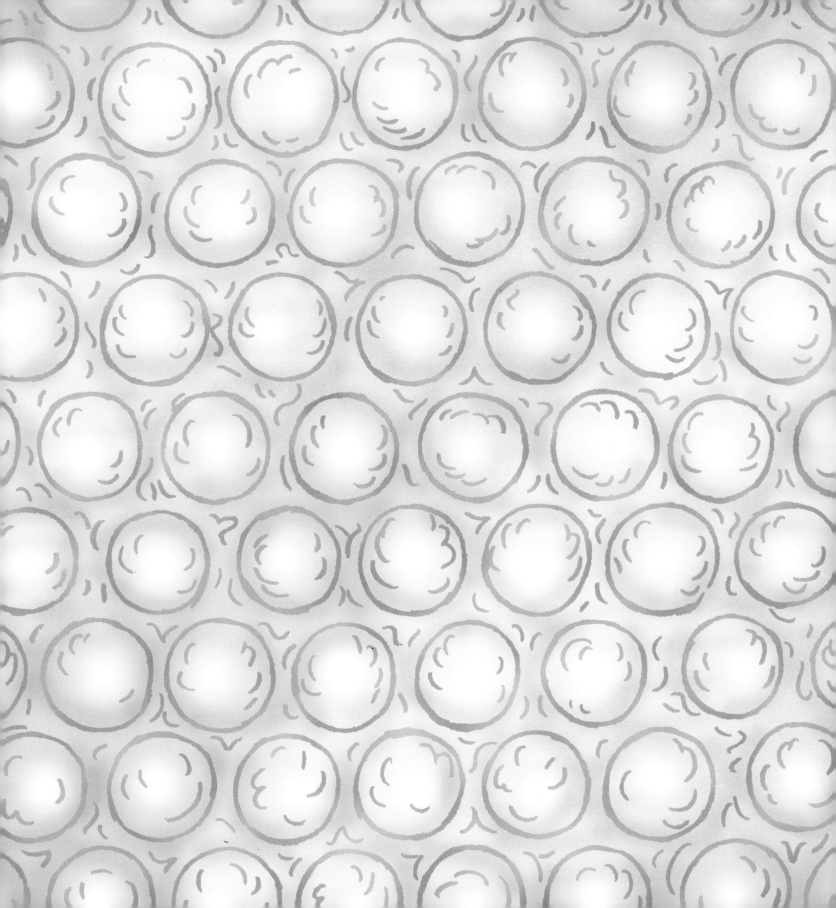

Bubble Wrap Girl

Written by Kari van Wakeren

Illustrated by CA Nobens

Edited by Lily Coyle
Illustrated by CA Nobens

ISBN: 978-1-59298-799-3
Library of Congress Catalog Number: 2017905080
Printed in the United States of America
First Printing: 2017
21 20 19 18 17   5 4 3 2 1

Beaver's Pond Press, Inc.
7108 Ohms Lane
Edina, MN 55439-2129

(952) 829-8818
www.BeaversPondPress.com

To order, visit www.ItascaBooks.com or call 1-800-901-3480 ext. 118.
Reseller discounts available.

To Thomas, Esme, and Reid—always and forever.

—K. V.

To Kaija, whom I'm proud of, for bravely trying new things.

—C. N.

Izzy Magee liked to do lots of different things, every day
of the week. She loved playing soccer and catch.
She loved to climb on the play set and play games at school.
She loved playing outside with her brother, Sam.

IZZY'S WEEK

Sunday	Monday	Tuesday	Wednesday
Visit Grandma and Grandpa	Hopscotch Tournament	Soccer Practice "⚽"	Bike Ride
Thursday	**Friday**	**Saturday**	
Picnic at the Park!	Playground	Dance Party ♫	

But there was one thing Izzy did not like at all.
Sometimes when Izzy was running around and having fun
doing things she enjoyed, she would get hurt.

On Sunday,
she whacked her back
while playing in the
treehouse with Sam.

On Monday, she tripped and skinned her knee as she played on the playground at school.

On Tuesday, she banged her hand on the counter as she ran to open the front door.

BANG!

On Wednesday, she lost her balance while riding her bike and bonked her funny bone.

BONK!

VOOM!

On Thursday, she stubbed her toe while she was dancing in the kitchen.

On Friday, she zoomed down the slide at the park so fast she landed hard on the ground.

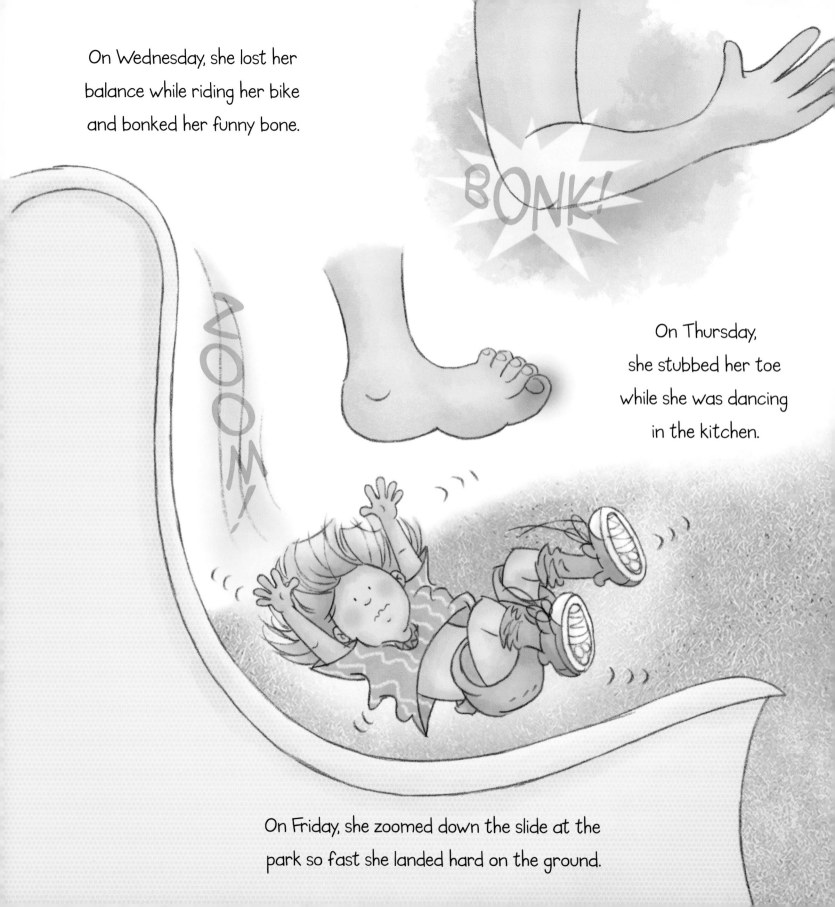

On Saturday, she slipped on the grass while running through the sprinkler.

Izzy did not like getting hurt at all.

So on Sunday, her parents wrapped her in bubble wrap before she went to her grandparents' house.

"Now, if you bump or scratch yourself while you are playing, you won't get hurt," said Mom.

Izzy didn't get hurt playing outside, but it was hard to pour lemonade at her lemonade stand.

On Monday, her parents wrapped her in bubble wrap before she went to school.

Izzy didn't get hurt when she accidentally knocked a chair over.

But it was hard
to raise her hand
when she knew
the answer
to her teacher's
question.

On Tuesday, her parents wrapped her
in bubble wrap before she went to soccer.
Izzy didn't get hurt when she and her teammate
smacked into each other.

But it was hard to kick the ball.

On Wednesday, her parents wrapped her in bubble wrap before she went outside to ride her bike. Izzy didn't get hurt when she knocked over the recyling in the garage.

But it was hard
to pedal.

On Thursday, her parents wrapped her
in bubble wrap before going to the park.
Izzy didn't get hurt when she bumped into Sam.

But she couldn't get up!
And she couldn't throw her
breadcrumbs far enough to
feed the ducks.

On Friday, her parents wrapped her in bubble wrap before she went to the playground.

Izzy didn't get hurt

on the teeter-totter.

But it was hard to swing
on the swings.

On Saturday,
her parents
wrapped her in
bubble wrap before
she went to a party.
(It covered up
her pretty
party dress.)

Izzy didn't get hurt when
Molly twirled into her.

But
it was
HARD
to do
the
Hokey
Pokey.

Izzy made a decision.

"Being wrapped in bubble wrap isn't any fun," she told her parents. "I don't get hurt as much, but it gets in the way of me doing the things I like to do!"

So she tore off the bubble wrap and ran out to play with Sam.

After that,
Izzy learned to ride her bike without training wheels.
She climbed to the top of the highest slide at the playground.
She jumped off the deep end at her friend's pool.

Izzy even played goalie during her soccer game.

She was proud of the new things she tried.

Izzy still sometimes got a bump or a bruise
on a Sunday or a Monday or a Tuesday
or a Wednesday or a Thursday
or a Friday or a Saturday.

But when she did,
Izzy got back up, brushed herself off,
and went on having fun.

ABOUT KARI VAN WAKEREN

In Kari's house, "Silly, Mommy!" is said a lot. In the midst of school and work, a typical day is filled with remembering, forgetting, cleaning up spills, doing laundry, sharing highs and lows, hugs, kisses, and lots of laughter. Kari is wowed by her kids daily, and the hopes and dreams she has for them inspire how she lives and what she writes.

ABOUT CA NOBENS

Little CA, the shortest kid in her kindergarten class, shot up like a weed in first grade. She didn't know where her head or her knees or her elbows began or ended, until she was the tallest girl in eighth grade. She was always clonking her noggin or stubbing her toe, or rapping her wrist or barking some bone on something. She could have used miles and miles of bubble wrap! Not having any, she just tried to stay still and draw pictures a lot.

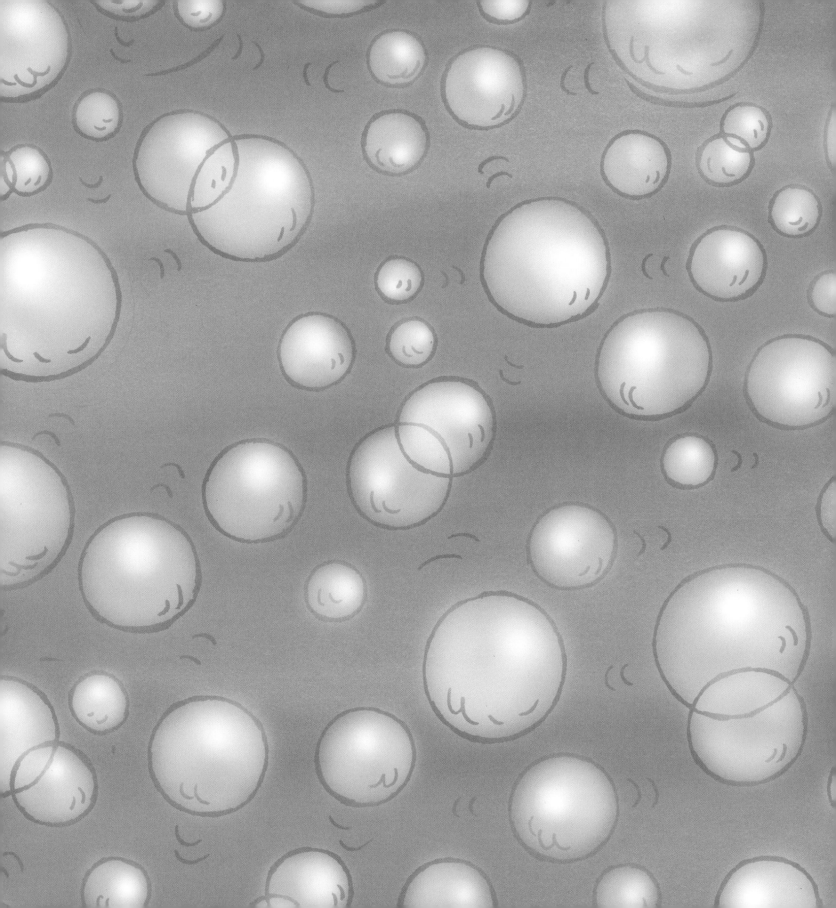

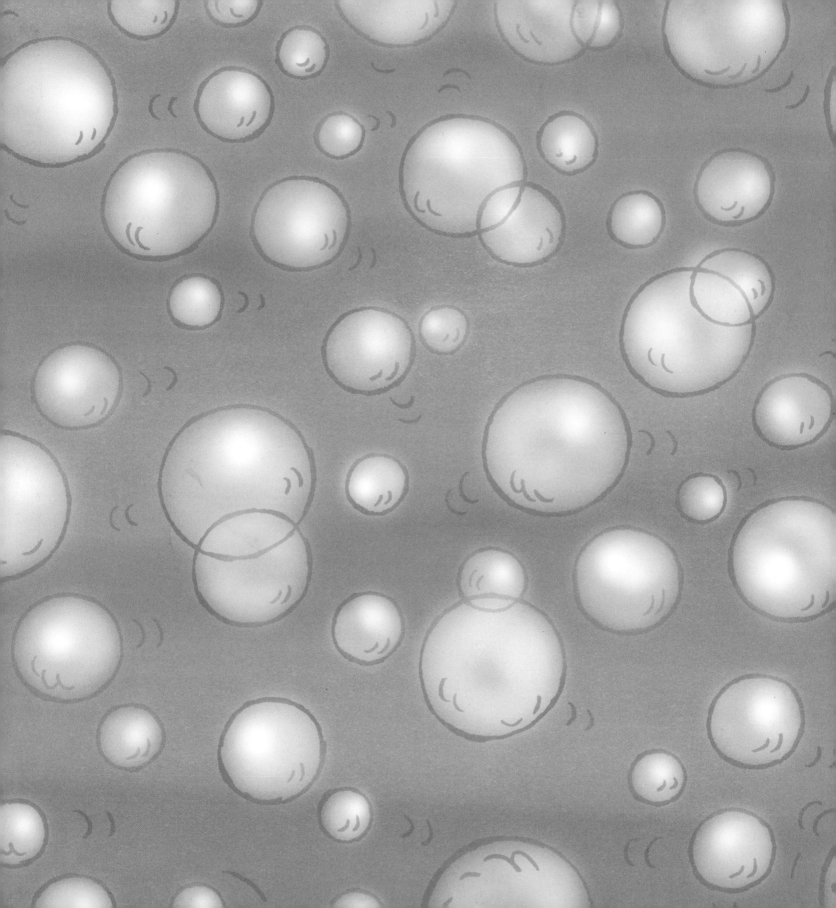